MY OH MY

Sweet Potato Pie

Love to Ella ♡, Beth + Bella

Beth Bloch

BETH BLOCH

DREAM CREEK PRESS

Ashland, Oregon

First Edition 2005

Publisher's Cataloging-In-Publication Data
(Prepared by The Donohue Group, Inc.)
Bloch, Beth.
My oh my, sweet potato pie / Beth Bloch. – 1st ed.
p. : ill. ; cm.
Summary: Miss Mattie's big dog Bella faces the temptation of
Aunt Lolly's sweet potato pies and must then win back the affections
of those she disappointed.
ISBN: 0-9771515-0-6
1. Interpersonal relations–Juvenile fiction. 2. Conduct of life–Juvenile fiction.
3. Dogs–Juvenile fiction. 4. Family life–Fiction.
5. Conduct of life–Fiction. 6. Dogs–Fiction. I. Title.
PS3552.L63 M96 2005
813.6/083   2005906679

Printed in Singapore

DREAM
CREEK
PRESS

401 Taylor Street • Ashland, Oregon 97520

Thank You!

To my mom, truly the best ever,
& in loving memory of my dad.
And of course to Bella,
my sweet companion & creative inspiration.

−*B.B.*

And Special Thanks to...

all of those who have loved,
supported, & encouraged me along
the way & helped me to get this
dream off the ground.

The day
MISS MATTIE
and her big dog
BELLA
went outside to work
so hard in the yard,

the spring

Sun

warmed them
and the air was filled
with the smell of
fresh dirt and
FLOWERS.

Miss Mattie loved Flowers.

She loved to plant them, smell them, and watch them grow.

BELLA LOVED FLOWERS TOO.

She loved to sniff them, dig them, and sometimes eat them.

The two friends began weeding here, planting there, digging

here and there, just as they did all the time.

Miss Mattie's friend Mr. Cal rode his bike by to say hi.

Crickets chirped. Birds sang.
After a While, the
Phone Rang
and broke the sounds of the country day.

It was Miss Mattie's Southern Aunt Lolly calling from her sister's in the city. "I've been travelin' all around and I'll be in your town soon! I'm comin' for a visit," she said with a drawl.

Aunt Lolly was arty, fun, and loved a party. She could also sometimes be a bit fussy and liked everything to be just right. Miss Mattie wondered what Aunt Lolly might think of Bella.

A LITTLE DROOL gathered at the corners of Bella's black lips. She had never met Aunt Lolly, but remembered her

Famous Sweet Potato Pies

she'd heard won a prize every year at the Southern Pie Jubilee. The last time Miss Mattie went for a visit to Aunt Lolly's, she returned home with a slice and gave Bella a lick that she could still almost **TASTE ON HER TONGUE.** There was much to prepare before Aunt Lolly got there. She would want everything to be just right. Miss Mattie scrubbed and mopped and swept and shined and scrubbed and mopped again. All the while, Bella helped.

AUNT LOLLY ARRIVED THE VERY NEXT DAY.
She opened the red door, and before she could set her bags on the floor, Bella bathed her with bad breath kisses. A big blonde tail almost wagged Aunt Lolly off her feet. Dog hair flew as Miss Mattie introduced the two.

My oh My

was all Aunt Lolly said.

Of course Aunt Lolly wanted a party to show off her sweet prized pies. A feast in the backyard would be just right. She and Miss Mattie made a list for the store. **WITH SAD EYES AND BIG SIGHS,** Bella begged to go. "Oh, no. You watch the house," Miss Mattie told her. Then she kissed Bella on the head, right in that soft spot on her brow, between her big brown orange eyes and said, **BYE BYE MY SWEET POTATO PIE,** just as she did all the time.

Back at home,
Smells of the
Feast

filled the house. Miss Mattie boiled
and cooked and peeled and chopped
and baked and cooked again.
BELLA WATCHED,
catching crumbs as they dropped.
All the while, Aunt Lolly worked
hard making her sweet potato pies,
rolling here, stirring there,
A PINCH OF SPICE
here and there, just as she did
all the time. She even slipped her
new friend Bella a taste or two
when Miss Mattie wasn't watching.
Soon there was enough food for
lots of hungry people...
OR ONE HUNGRY DOG.

The guests began to arrive at five.

BELLA HAD LICKS FOR EVERYONE.

Bella eyed the grill,

smelled the smells and tasted some treats from Mr. Cal.

UNDER THE TABLE,

tangled among the legs and feet,

Bella listened to the sounds of the party...

until she heard another sound,

Miss Mattie's voice in her head saying

"Bye bye my sweet potato pie."

THEN BELLA HAD A THOUGHT.

"I bet I can make those pies go bye bye."

The idea made her lips quiver and her tongue curl.

Drool began to drip down her furry, yellow chin.

Bella slowly

Slipped

Away...

When the food was gone and the talk was mostly done, **AUNT LOLLY WENT TO THE KITCHEN** to fetch her famous pies. She was silly with excitement to hea everyone's kind replies. Instead Aunt Lolly cried, horrified...

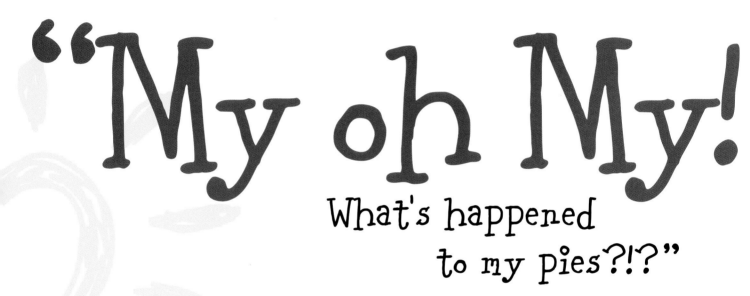

"My oh My!

What's happened to my pies?!?"

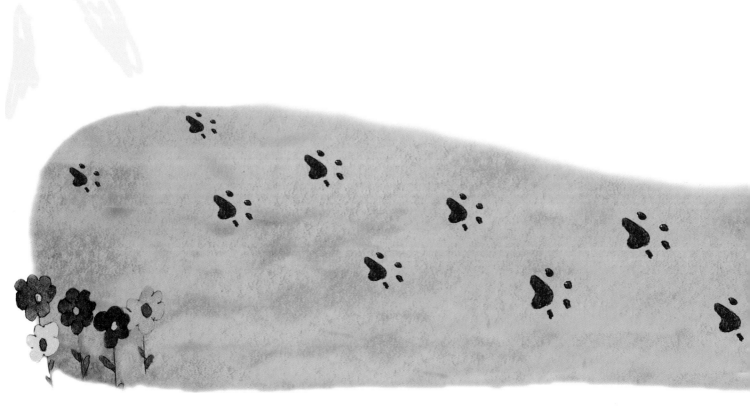

Miss Mattie and Mr.Cal led the way.
They ran to the kitchen to see what was wrong!

Aunt Lolly could not even look at Bella's sweet, furry face

all covered in Mush.

She was not feeling too fond of Bella right now. Aunt Lolly could take no more. **FEELING FUSSY** and frazzled, she stomped her feet up the stairs, sighed **MY OH MY** and slammed the bedroom door!

When the guests left, poor Miss Mattie was left with all that mess. Mr. Cal stayed long enough to help. They scrubbed and mopped and swept and shined and scrubbed and mopped again. When all was done and Mr. Cal said goodbye, Miss Mattie was ready to drop.

Bella wriggled in her bed.

Her belly Rumbled

and Tumbled

from too much pie and her brown orange eyes wanted to cry.
Miss Mattie could not stay mad at Bella for long.

YOU'RE STILL MY SWEET POTATO PIE,

she whispered.

Bella hated to have made Aunt Lolly mad.
So the next morning she rose with the sun.
SHE RUSHED TO THE YARD
where she and Miss Mattie had worked so hard.
Bella sniffed out her favorite flowers and
DUG A BIG BUNCH
for Aunt Lolly. She gathered them in her mouth
and trotted inside, muddy paws and all.

There at the table sat Aunt Lolly and Miss Mattie,
sipping their breakfast tea.

Bella plopped the
Slobbered

flowers all covered with dirt right at Aunt Lolly's feet.
"My oh my," Aunt Lolly exclaimed, splashing her tea in the air.

Aunt Lolly wanted to be mad, but she liked the flower bunch so much! When she looked down at the mess it made, she **WANTED TO STOMP** her feet and feel all fussy. She was still mad about those messed up pies. She wanted to turn her head away in dismay. Instead...

she felt her

Heart

grow big and a smile move across her face.

And when it came time to pack her bags and
head back home, a lump came to her throat.
I'M GONNA MISS YA'LL,
she said with a drawl. Then she hugged Miss Mattie
so tight. "Come see me down South real soon!"

But before she could go, Aunt Lolly

Kissed Bella on the head,

right in that soft spot on her brow,
between her big brown orange eyes and said,
BYE BYE MY SWEET POTATO PIE.

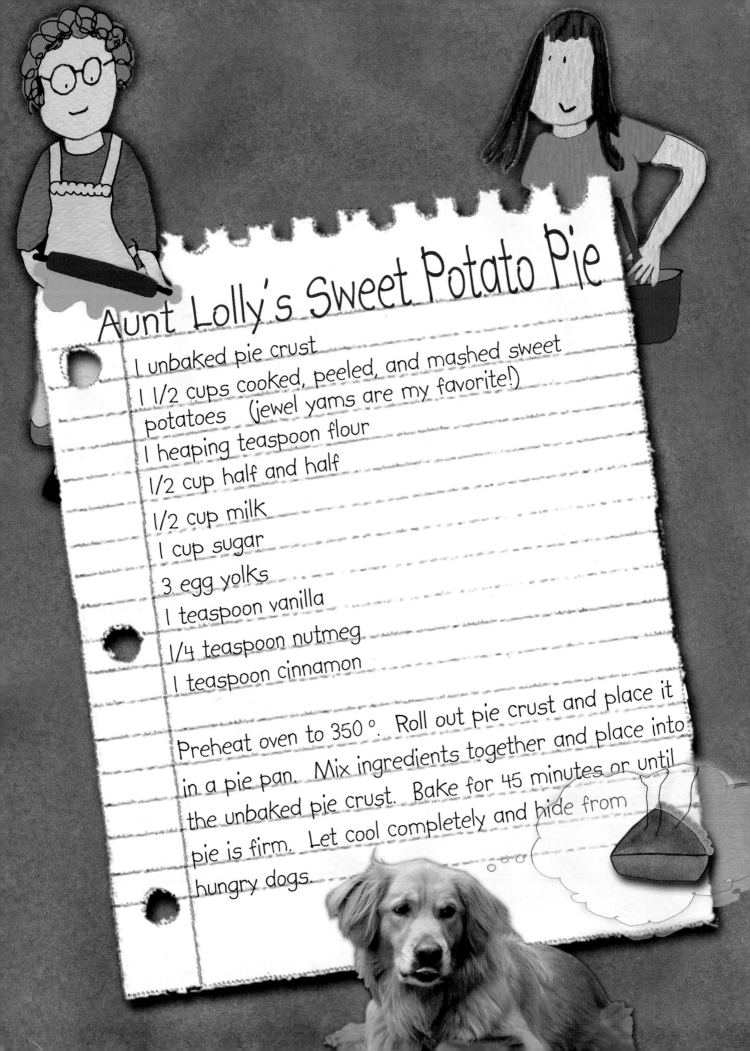

Aunt Lolly's Sweet Potato Pie

1 unbaked pie crust

1 1/2 cups cooked, peeled, and mashed sweet potatoes   (jewel yams are my favorite!)

1 heaping teaspoon flour

1/2 cup half and half

1/2 cup milk

1 cup sugar

3 egg yolks

1 teaspoon vanilla

1/4 teaspoon nutmeg

1 teaspoon cinnamon

Preheat oven to 350°. Roll out pie crust and place it in a pie pan. Mix ingredients together and place into the unbaked pie crust. Bake for 45 minutes or until pie is firm. Let cool completely and hide from hungry dogs.